NOVEL TITLES
BY RENEE GOODWIN

Living Past Shadows

GG LIFE LESSON STORYBOOK SERIES ®
BY RENEE GOODWIN

GG Cleans House – Learning Teamwork
GG Meets Her Match – Becoming Forever Friends
GG Asks, "Is Jesus In Your Class?" – Seek, Know, Guide, Inspire
GG Takes Action – Practicing Health Safety

A Love, A Life
Forgone

A Love, A Life Forgone

Renee Goodwin

Goodwin Global
Publishing

GOODWIN GLOBAL PUBLISHING, LLC
TYLER, TEXAS

Copyright © 2022 by Renee Goodwin
All rights reserved.
First Edition

Goodwin Global Publishing, LLC
Tyler, TX

Published by Goodwin Global Publishing, LLC 2022

ISBN 979-8-9869964-3-1 (paperback)
ISBN 979-8-9869964-4-8 (digital)

Cover artwork by Renee Goodwin
Book layout and design by Gabriela Fleming
Author photograph by Diana Cassetta-Perez

Printed in the United States of America

dedication

For my husband and sons, who were
instrumental in the creation of
Goodwin Global Publishing, LLC.

A Love, A Life Forgone

table of contents

chapter one

My emotions were overflowing as I made my way back to the house. We had a family BBQ at the picnic area by the smokehouse and reminisced of the years gone by. It was getting late in the afternoon, time for everyone to return to their lives. My three daughters, their husbands and children departed in three different directions. Lucy and Clark with baby Carter went southeast back to Nashville, Tennessee. Lacey and Wayne headed northeast to New York City with one-year old Henry and Lexie and Niccolò went east to the D.C. area with sons Ricardo, Lorenzo, and Antonio. I was still in Kansas, trying to hold myself together.

Once inside, I took a moment to catch my breath, contemplating sitting in my comfy chair by the window for a few minutes rest. The last few days with the family visiting had been a whirlwind to describe it mildly. All had come to honor the anniversary of the passing of my beloved husband, Hank, their father and grandfather. It had been a sad, happy few days together.

I met Hank Gray at a BBQ cook-off in 1985. I was hesitant at the time but my neighbors insisted that I come with them to the cook-off event. Hank locked eyes on me in the audience and motioned for me to join him on the cooking platform. Hank gave me my assignment to make BBQ sauce right there on the spot. For years, I teased Hank, "You were a lucky Pit-master that day." I happened to know the secret ingredient for an incredible BBQ sauce, add a splash of Worcestershire. Yes, we were the winning team and remained winners throughout our married life.

To describe our relationship, Hank was a wonderful, kind man, awesome father, and always supportive of me and our daughters. I knew Hank adored me and I adored him back. We enjoyed each other's company. We had a very happy relationship yet a very predictable relationship. What you saw was what you got. It was all good, but that deep, share your inner soul love with each other was non-existent. And, I always wished it could have been.

There really were no lows in our relationship. And the true highs of our relationship, of course, were the birth of our daughters. I guess you could say becoming the 1985 Kansas City BBQ Competition Grand Champion Pit-masters established our lifelong path together. From there, every weekend was spent competing or tweaking our sauce recipe before the next competition.

Hank and I married in 1987. We exchanged vows in the local church chapel with a few friends in attendance. The reception or to this day, as most refer to it, "The Shindig" began. Live country-western music, boot stomping dancing and the main features, BBQ, BBQ, BBQ. My friends teased me about marrying Hank. You see, my maiden name was Agnes Brown. Now, my name was changing to Agnes Gray. Switching from Brown to Gray, I felt like a box of crayons. I am not sure I have ever gotten used to my last name.

With Hank, I knew BBQ would be my destiny and I accepted that path. Hank and I opened HG's BBQ. I personally never cared for the name. To me, the name was not very creative or original but it worked. People came from all around and even from out of state to taste HG's BBQ. HG's BBQ smokehouse was located next door to our home. I was able to help Hank cook 24/7 and still raise our family.

We were blessed with three daughters; Lucy, Lacey and Lexie. The girls were all born two years apart. For a few years, it was a three-ring circus most days, yet happy and memorable days. Time passed swiftly. One minute the girls were playing house, the next minute they were getting married, but in reverse order.

Lexie, the youngest always informed the family that she was not interested in getting married, that she had many adventures ahead for herself. As you guessed, Lexie was the first of the three to marry. Lexie met Niccolò while studying abroad in Rome, Italy. Before we knew it, Hank, Lucy, Lacey and I were touring Vatican City, meeting wonderful people and I was definitely enjoying the Italian cuisine (for a few days, no BBQ, hallelujah).

The wedding was absolutely beautiful. The ceremony was a catholic mass celebrated in an "ah" inspiring cathedral in the center of Rome. The cathedral arches soared up toward the sky. The music from the pipe organ filled the air with Mendelssohn's *The Wedding March.*

The reception was held in the countryside on Niccolò's family estate. The view, the people, and yes, the food and wine were all magnificent and never-ending. The label on one of the wines being served caught my eye. The label had the letter "L" uniquely inscribed in the upper right corner. Along with the inscription, there was a scene of a sailboat cruising along the shoreline. For some reason, the picture seemed familiar to me. That is when I decided I best finish the occasion with glasses of water.

Lexie and Niccolò were so in love, so happy. I was able to return home with peace in my heart. Soon afterwards, we learned that with Lexie and Niccolò working in International Affairs, planning their future, they felt it best to move to the states. Decided to locate outside of Washington, D.C. where they would be able to continue their work and start their family.

Shortly after Lexie's wedding, Lacey announces she is engaged to Wayne. After college, Lacey moved to

New York City to follow a career in investment banking. Lacey loved the big city life and flourished the moment she arrived. She rented an adorable apartment near her work. She told me she met a really nice guy in 3B down the hall from her apartment. The next minute I get a call from Lacey, "Wayne asked me to marry him." Without hesitation Lacey added, "I said, yes!"

This time, Hank, Lucy and I traveled to New York City. What an eye-opener! I can get around in a big city, but a metropolis is not for me.

The wedding ceremony, similar to Lexie's wedding, was a catholic mass celebrated at a beautiful cathedral near Lacey and Wayne's apartment complex. I could go on and on about the magnificent stain glass windows in the cathedral. The light of day shining through the windows showed the brilliant stain glass colors. I will always remember Lacey and Wayne standing in front of the altar professing their faith and love for each other.

The reception was held on the rooftop of the investment bank building where Lacey and Wayne worked. What a sight! You could see New York City in a "360 degree" panoramic view. It was magnificent! The food and wine were exceptional as well. It was odd, but I thought I recognized the same wine being served as at Lexie's reception. The wine bottle had the same "L" inscription on the label but with a scene of a tropical beach shore. Again, for some reason, the picture seemed familiar to me. I immediately switched to drinking water the rest of the evening. I truly enjoyed the wedding but I was truly ready to get home. The constant motion became too much hustle and bustle for me.

The days had barely simmered down when Lucy called from Nashville telling me about Clark. Apparently, Clark was an attorney working with the same law firm as Lucy except Clark's office was on the fourth floor and Lucy's office was on the third floor. Lucy was bubbling over telling me her story, I was trying to keep up. Apparently, Clark had seen Lucy in the building cafeteria and it was love at first sight for both.

Lucy said they were planning a spring wedding. Which at first sounded reasonable. Then she announced the date March 19th. Yikes, six weeks. Lucy explained, within the catholic religion, during Lent, you could only have a wedding ceremony on a feast day. March 19th is the Feast Day of St. Joseph. Lucky for us, March 19th that year was on a Saturday.

So, Hank and I met the family in Nashville. Lacey and Wayne came from New York while Lexie, Niccolò and family traveled from D.C. I don't believe the girls were competing however, I am here to say the cathedral in Nashville was breathtaking. From the moment I walked in, my spirit overflowed with God's grace and mercy. I had not had the opportunity to spend much time getting to know Clark. I was comforted hearing Lucy and Clark exchange their vows. I knew they would share a special love.

The reception was held at the country club associated with the law firm where Lucy and Clark practiced. The ballroom was decorated so elegantly. There was dinner and endless country music and dancing. Steak and potatoes were the main entrée on the menu. (Thank goodness for beef, but not BBQ). I really thought my emotions were getting the best of me when I saw the wine label on the bottles of wine being served. It was the same wine served at Lexie's reception and Lacey's but this time the label had the same "L" inscription but the scene was of horses running on the beach. The picture and inscription seemed familiar to me again. At that point, I decided that was my last glass of wine for the evening. So, I set my sights on cake. I would never admit this to Lexie and Lacey, but Lucy's wedding cakes were delicious. I had seconds. Being the "Mother of the Bride" has a few perks!

Hank and I were very proud of our daughters. As they were growing up, we escaped HG's BBQ as often was we could to devote family time for the girls. For most outings we visited museums, a common interest of all. We immersed ourselves in art, natural history, agriculture, architecture, and science. I believe those days of enrichment inspired the girls to pursue their careers. All three are professionals in their own right. I also believe they will be loving wives and wonderful, caring mothers. Hank and I knew the girls were financially sound and would be safe and secure with their loving husbands and families.

With the girls happily married and their families beginning to grow, Hank and I thought we would settle in for a few more years of HG's BBQ, then try retirement. We were planning to move to a nearby lake. Hank wanted to fish. He mentioned building a smokehouse changing his main entrée from beef to fish. Seeing the look on my face as he began to share his smokehouse plans with me, he quickly changed his mind. Hank said Agnes, "I think I will just catch and release." I smiled and nodded in reply, "Great idea!"

Hank and I changed the HG's BBQ smokehouse schedule to weekends only, 10:00 am to 4:00 pm or until all the BBQ was gone. That happened usually by 2:00 pm. Hank and I were enjoying our weekdays, getting into a daily routine, morning coffee, newspaper and book reading, and listening to our favorite songs. I still had my vinyl records and player. Our conversations ventured past buying brisket and ribs and storing up firewood. The days showed promise.

One morning Hank didn't feel like stoking up fire in the smokehouse. He told me he would tend to it later. Immediately, I knew something was wrong. Stoking the fire in the smokehouse was Hank's first order of business every day. Hank walked slowly to the sunroom with his coffee, sat in his favorite chair and breathed his last breath.

I panicked. Hank was not breathing and had no pulse. I called 911 and began CPR as instructed, 30 chest compressions then 2 rescue breaths. I was screaming, begging Hank to come back. But Hank was gone. When the paramedics arrived, they pulled me away taking me in the next room while they cared for Hank. Oh, my Hank was gone. Oh, my Hank was gone. It was the Lord's turn to enjoy Hank. Oh, my Hank was gone.

I did not want to accept that my life with Hank had ended, that Hank would not be by my side. I kept the smokehouse fired up cooking BBQ at HG's, for a while but that didn't bring Hank back. I tried to improve our signature BBQ sauce but that didn't bring Hank back. Finally, I hung the "We Are Closed" sign on the smokehouse door. I had to face reality. Hank could not be by my side. Hank was not coming back. I was alone.

I knew I needed to get a grip on myself, and fast. I was rapidly falling into the depths of no return. I felt my life was an empty stage since Hank was no longer with me day to day. I knew my surroundings had to change. I was not sure if moving to the lake as Hank and I were planning would be the right decision. I was afraid every day I would be talking to him as if he was still there saying, "Hank, I caught two bass this morning. I think they were four pounders. I let them go." I could see Hank smiling back at me and laughing saying, "Agnes, together the two may have weighed four pounds. I wish I could have helped you reel them in." Those types of mental conversations were inevitable unless I made some drastic lifestyle adjustments.

chapter two

I moved to the mountains. The scenery, the air, the temperature, everything was different. I had not realized the majority of my life I had lived on level terrain. Now I was surrounded by hills, valleys, mountains. It seemed I was closer to the sun.

Looking back, I realize it was an extreme move but I was desperate. I had to make a change. There was an older couple, the Morrisons, wanting to downsize and move closer to their children and families. The mountains were getting too steep for their elderly years. Not to say I am a spring chicken but, the Morrisons had lived a few decades of life more than me.

Maybe I should have considered moving closer to Lucy, Lacey or Lexie. In my heart of hearts, I felt I would have been a burden so I found my way to the mountains. The Morrisons asked for one favor. They had a dog named, Rusty. He was a Bernese Mountain Dog. The Morrisons were moving to the coast. They felt Rusty would not be able to acclimate to the heat and humidity so the Morrisons asked if I would adopt Rusty.

Of course, I did not hesitate to agree. I welcomed Rusty with open arms. For so many years, all my attentions were given to Hank, the girls and HG's BBQ. Our family did not have a pet. Now, I was blessed with Rusty. He was an awesome dog. The Morrisons had trained him well. Rusty was obedient yet full of life. Just what I needed, a life restoration.

I remember a time in my early life so to speak when I needed a life restoration. I was several years working in my career as a corporate liaison. I negotiated mergers between large and small corporations. The work was grueling yet fascinating at the same time. Unfortunately, there was never an off switch, unless you walked away for a while.

I was feeling a daily mental fatigue, trudging through life. Time away from the daily grind I hoped would be the magic I needed. So, I planned my first vacation. I had money saved to be able to go anywhere, within reason, and stay for about a month.

Perusing brochure after brochure, I was lured to location offering a private house on the beach. The photos on the brochure showed gentle waves rolling in on the beach shores as the sun set on the horizon. There was one photo of a beautiful waterfall cascading down into a fresh pool of water. There were photos of the home, actually given a closer look, it appeared to be a cottage shaded by palm trees with a white picket fence surrounding the perimeter. The photos of the tropical flowers with such colorful blooms were splendid.

The next day I booked the trip. A few weeks later I was on my way to paradise. Upon arrival, the brochures were true to their advertising. The tropical flowers were gorgeous but what the brochure couldn't share was the sensational aromas, the sweet smells surrounding at all times. The cottage with the white picket fence was true to its photo. I couldn't wait for the sun to set to absorb the array of light as it disappears beyond the horizon.

To my surprise, an added bonus the brochure didn't mention, the kitchen was fully stocked with fresh juices and fruits, vegetables, breads and meats. I was set for the month. Not a care in the world. Truthfully, I admit it took a few days to detox from the world I left behind. But then it was just me and the world in front of me to fully explore.

As I was winding down the first few days, I stayed close to the cottage, soaking in the sunrise, relaxing in the hammock watching the palm trees sway. I swam morning, noon and night. In the water I felt so light, floating in and out with the waves. It was my paradise, my life restoration, and more.

One day I decided to venture into the small town. There was a bicycle on the back porch of the cottage but I thought for the first trek, I would walk. The brochure suggested it was an easy walk to town. The brochure was right again. Ten minutes later I was browsing the local shops. I forgot to pack a straw hat and my freckles were popping out even after slathering my face with sunscreen.

At the end of the street, a lady was weaving some beautiful straw hats with different sized brims. I asked her to show me a hat with an extra wide brim. From her collection, I picked a hat accented with pink ribbon woven around the brim. I tried it on. It was a perfect fit. Now, I walked along full of tropical style and spirit.

I always felt seafood was such a delicacy so I rarely ordered fish, shrimp, or lobster when dining out. And, I rarely cooked it at home either. It seemed the smell of the fresh catch of the day stayed in my apartment for weeks. But now while in paradise, with this tropical breeze, why not?

Walking from town toward the beach I smelled fish cooking on the grill. Following the enticing aroma, I came upon a small hut surrounded by palm trees. The hut was actually a restaurant serving grilled fish and advertising bar drink specials. Again, I thought, why not? I have never been an adult beverage drinker but, the umbrella-drink the guy next to me was slurping looked appealing. Tapping him on his shoulder I asked, "Your drink looks so refreshing, what is it?" As soon as the words came out of my mouth, I was so embarrassed. How lame! Why didn't I act somewhat educated and say, "That looks like a Martini, shaken not stirred." Then, when he turned around, I really wanted to crawl under the bar. I should have just asked the bartender for a Tequila Sunrise, Rum Punch, or some type of tropical sounding drink and continued on my way.

"The locals call it the Painkiller."

"I see."

Yikes, this could turn into a dangerous conversation so I turned back to the bartender.

"I will have a Shirley Temple.

I heard the guy beside me chuckle. I tried to turn my back to him.

"Shirley Temple is a little on the light side, don't you think."

"Maybe so, but I am happy to report I don't have any pain to kill at the moment."

The bartender served my drink. I grabbed it swiftly and headed to the beach not looking back. I thought it best to forgo ordering food at the moment. Sitting watching the sunset catching my breath from the awkward bar scene, I reflected on "The Guy."

Dating had not been my thing. I was more interested in my studies, graduating and pursuing my career(s). I consider myself friendly but reserved. I had a life agenda that didn't match those around me. I admit I really wanted to do a double take. Those blue eyes, thick black hair and tanned complexion were breathtaking. With that tan, I wonder if he is a local.

Oh well, now that that little thrill was over, I took a big sip of my Shirley Temple wishing it was what they call a Dirty Shirley Temple. I turned my gaze to the sea and absorbed the colors of the setting sun.

"Hello, I think we met briefly at the bar moments ago."

I about fell out of my sling back chaise lounge.

"Yes, hello!" Could not think of anything else to say. Ugh!

"I didn't mean to scare you with my Painkiller. The name is more serious than the drink."

"I will just take your word on that."

"No, seriously, it is the truth. Want a sip?"

"Still sounds too dangerous for me. I am a light-weight. I will stick to my Shirley Temple."

"Do you mind if I join you?" "The Guy" pointed to the chaise lounge beside me.

"Sure, it is not taken. Help yourself." My voice was quivering.

"My name is Mark, Mark Stoneleigh." Thank goodness I can stop thinking of him as "The Guy." But do I really want to know his name and more?

"Nice to meet you, again, I joked." My name is Grace Brownley, I stuttered sheepishly."

My real name, the name on my birth certificate is

Agnes Brown. Oh, why couldn't I have a more interesting name. My mother's given name was Francesca Conti. How beautiful! I am sorry for her sake and mine that she had to relinquish her maiden name for Brown. But really, mom and dad, Agnes. For years, I begged my parents to rename me. But they loved the name "Agnes." To me, Agnes is a name one has to constantly live up to. It is so strong and mature. So, I never feel I can let my hair down.

Well now is the time. This is the place. I am letting my hair down. As I meet new friends on my vacation, I will be Grace Brownley. No harm done.

"Grace, have you been at this paradise retreat long?" he asked.

"Ah, Grace! Did you hear me?"

I have got to get use to my new name.

"I arrived a few days ago. This is my first trip to town."

"I booked a little place up the beach for the summer. I have a few weeks remaining on my rental," he offered.

"I rented a cottage down the way. So far, so good." Why am I at a loss for words? Seriously! I negotiate for a living. If anyone can keep a conversation going, it is me. I guess I have let Mark shake my sandals.

"I manage a family business back in the states. And you?"

"Oh, I deal in mergers." I thought that career description I gave him sounded professional but not over the top. Truthfully, I wanted to impress him but not come across too haughty.

In my limited encounters with men outside the workplace and in the workplace, I have discovered it is a major turn-off to them if they feel women professionals are more intelligent and accomplished than themselves. This little tidbit works in my favor. When I sense a guy is developing an inferiority complex just trying to talk to me that is my sign to say, "Adios!" I have learned cutting my losses short proves best for all in the end, especially for me.

"That sounds interesting. Have you dealt in mergers long?"

"A few years. How long have you helped with your families' business?" Oh my! This conversation is going nowhere fast.

"A while. I see you have finished your drink. Would you care for another one?"

"No, thank you, I am fine." I knew I should not intake any more sugar. I was shaking as it was.

"Would you like to walk along the beach with me?"

"That sounds wonderful." As I made my way out of my lounge chair, my knees buckled. Maybe there was alcohol in my drink. No, I was super excited. Mark caught me before I ate a bucket full of sand. "Thank you.

I am usually more sure-footed. I guess I am not used to these sandals," I explained as my cover-up. I wonder if he believed me?

chapter three

The paradise retreat brochure listed a number of activities highlighting scuba diving, snorkeling, horseback riding on the beach, biking and hiking in the mountain area and sunset dinner sailing. Physically, I consider myself of average weight and height being five foot, five inches tall. I have always thought I was agile and coordinated. I marched and played the flute in the band during my high school years. Now, actually looking at the mountain towering straight up in the middle of this paradise retreat seemed too intimating for my biking abilities. I may consider a hike, though?

The scuba diving excursions required lessons and checkout dives which all seemed too intensive for this trip. During future trips if such trips came to be, then scuba diving could be an option.

Now, I had always dreamed of riding horses on the beach. I enjoy movie scenes where young lovers gallop along the shoreline, horse hooves splashing through the sea. These movie scenes exude a sense of freedom and peace. Yes, I was sold on a day of horseback riding. The dinner sail was enticing as well.

In my travel preparations, I counseled myself, "Agnes, don't plan every minute of each day. Just let it happen." Remembering my own words of advice, the next morning I went for a swim and let the rest of the day happen.

It happened alright! I ventured to town to sign up for horseback riding. I paid my deposit and the tour guide said, "Grace Brownley, you are set, tomorrow morning 10:00 am." I started to correct him thinking he had me confused with another guest. But I remembered I was traveling under my pseudo name. The guide suggested, "The morning rides were cooler." Appreciative of his recommendation, I replied, "Thank you. Sounds wonderful, I can't wait."

While in town, my mind played the "Yes, No Game". Yes, I should entertain the idea of another Shirley Temple, hoping, wishing to run into Mark, again. No, I have finished my errand in town, just go back to the cottage. Well, I am thirsty and it is five o'clock somewhere. Yes, I will go by the paradise bar on my way back to the cottage. Deal, yes, no?

Arriving at the paradise bar, there was no sign of Mark. I guess I was disappointed but relieved at the same time. I thanked the bartender for my usual and walked to the beach to enjoy my Shirley Temple and the sunset. The sunsets never disappoint. The array of colors captivates while the sun slowly disappears beyond the horizon. During times as these, I wish I was a better photographer. Before the trip, I splurged on the newest and greatest camera; Minolta X-700. The salesclerk excitedly explained the features; aperture, shutter speed, self-timer, flash sink…He stopped abruptly seeing my eyes glazed over from the show and tell. He said, "Miss, I set it on "A" for automatic and you are good to go."

"Perfect, thank you." As I was checking out, paying for the camera and few accessories the salesclerk decided I needed, I thought this little splurge may cost more than the vacation. Oh well! I hope I don't accidentally move the setting off of "A".

Working fast, yet carefully, not wanting to miss a minute of photographing the sunset, I pulled the camera from its special case in my backpack. Great, the camera made it through my travels so far and was still set on "A". I took off the lens cover and began snapping picture after picture of the setting sun.

"It is an awesome view."

I almost dropped my costly camera into the sea.

"Yes, it is." Here I go with my three-word replies. Get a grip, Agnes. It was Mark! "I hope I have a few good shots."

"With this beautiful scenery, every picture will be fantastic!"

"Let's hope."

He is not aware of my lack of photography skills. Hopefully I can keep it a secret like my pseudo name.

"I don't want to interrupt your photography session, but I was going to grab a fish sandwich at a small place down the beach. Care to join me?"

"That sounds like fun." My heart beating out of my chest, palms sweating almost dropping the camera again. Mark caught the camera strap just before the camera plunged into the sand.

"Great save!" Mark examines my camera.

"I have a camera similar to yours."

Yea! We have something in common.

"My camera is a Nikon FE2. It operates like your Minolta, but it does not have the automatic feature. I like to change the settings for each picture."

Sure, he does.

I managed to get the camera safely back in the case. Changing the subject quickly, I announce, "I am ready, show me the way."

chapter four

The next morning, I hurried dressing. I didn't want to be late for my beach horseback ride. I was bubbling over with anticipation. I hope I don't disappoint myself. Not thinking of riding horses when I was packing, a pair of jeans did make it to my suitcase with a long-sleeved blouse and tennis shoes. Originally, I considered packing only bathing suits and flip-flops. Thank goodness rationality eased into the suitcase.

While eating with Mark the day before, I let him know I was signed up for the morning horseback ride. All the while I was hoping he may have taken the hint. When, I arrived, there was no sign of Mark.

The horseback riding excursion was all I dreamed of and more. The morning ride welcomed a cool breeze the horses and myself enjoyed. My horse's name was Wildfire, a red and white dappled Mustang. Wildfire loved to gallop through the sea. Wildfire and I stayed at the back of the group so we could splash to our hearts delight. I believe that was the most fun I have ever had.

So free, so alive. I laughed and Wildfire whinnied as we turned to journey back to the stables.

Suddenly, I took a double take. Could that be Mark walking from that humongous home, black rod iron gates with a mile long driveway? I thought he said he rented a little place up the beach. If this is little to him, I wonder what he considers big.

Wildfire and I did an about face to take another look. That was Mark alright. Wow! Of course, my imagination started running wild. Is he a millionaire, a silver spoon, a spoiled brat? Funny, he doesn't come across as any of those types. Or have I just been blinded and wooed by his good looks and calm demeanor. As the bible professes, I best gird my loins.

Have I totally misinterpreted this interlude?

With my slight detour, I got separated from the horseback riding group. I was not worried about being lost; Wildfire took me directly back to the barn. I dismounted, gave Wildfire a huge kiss and thanked him for the memorable ride…then I remembered Mark and the palace. Learning this bit of information, I can assume Mark most probably is way out of my league. I need to refocus and remember why I am on this vacation; to relax, to enjoy, not find my forever love.

Gathering my things, the tour guide asked if I would like to join the group the next day for a hiking excursion.

"Sure, why not!"

"Then, Grace, we will see you at 10. If you need hiking boots, we can furnish you a pair."

Remembering I had only packed tennis shoes and flip-flops I replied, "I look forward to the hike. Thank you, I believe I will take you up on that boot offer, size 7 please. See you in the morning."

I was extremely hungry from the ride. Do I dare go get a fish sandwich? What if Mark is there? What will I say? Saw you and your little rented castle today. Oh, Agnes, just forget about all of that and enjoy your lunch.

Scanning the sandwich shop, all clear. There was no sign of Mark. The sandwich I ordered the day before was spectacular. I decided to order it again but with homemade chips this time.

"It looks like you have been riding."

Oh my gosh, it was Mark! "Yes, Wildfire and I had a great ride."

"I saw the group ride by this morning. Was that you at the back of the group?"

"Yes, Wildfire really likes to splash! I thought the back of the pack was best."

"I am sure the others appreciated your kind gesture."

"I hope so. I would have much rather been at the front, seeing everything first."

"Oh, so you are an over achiever, the assertive type."

Ah! Mark is showing his true colors. I guess he is the male dominating type after all. Looks like this little infatuation, romance or whatever you want to call it I had going on in my head is coming to a quick halt. "I beg your pardon. Are you calling me an over achiever? Maybe I should be calling you money pockets?"

"What are you talking about?"

"The little place you rented up the beach is a palace. Wildfire and I saw you there this morning. It takes boo-coo dollars to afford those accommodations for the summer."

"That place is a palace, but that is not where I am staying."

"It's not?"

"No, that residence belongs to a very friendly couple I met when I first arrived. As we were talking that day, we discovered we all shared a love for flowers. Their home is surrounded by indigenous plants blooming all year. The blooms from their plants in their gardens are very aromatic. They offered for me to cut fresh flowers for me to have at my place anytime."

"Oh." My heart sank. This is where I wish I would have kept my mouth shut. Why did I have to call him money pockets? What a goof I am! I need to apologize, tuck my tail and run. "That was very nice of the couple to share their flowers with you. I apologize for speaking out of turn. Well, I just finished my lunch. I need to be on my way. Bye!"

Before he had a chance to speak, I grabbed my things and darted up the path, not looking back. What a blunder I created. It is a sure bet I will never cross paths with Mark again. Why did I have to blow it? I really liked him. Why, Agnes, why?

chapter five

Trying not to let my money pocket faux pas spoil my vacation I turned my attentions to the beauty surrounding me. I saw a photo shop. I was hoping they would be able to develop the pictures I had taken so far. I let the clerk remove the film from my camera. The clerk, a young man looked at me strangely as if wondering and questioning why didn't I remove the film myself.

To answer his puzzled look, I confessed, "I am an "automatic photographer." I appreciate you removing the film for me. I most likely would expose the film if I tried." He smiled and carried on. The clerk said he could have the pictures ready in a few minutes so I waited. As he handed me my photos I sheepishly asked, "Would you please reload the camera and make sure it is set on "A" for me? The "A" is for automatic. Thank you." He loaded the camera so I could watch and learn. Realizing his efforts were all for not, he rolled his eyes, handed me the camera saying with exhaustion, "You are welcome."

Sitting at the beach, soaking up some well needed rays of sun my nine to five corporate indoor environment body rarely experiences, enjoying the tropical breeze, I looked through my package of photos. When I get home, I will create a photo album to have on my coffee table to remind me of this beautiful place.

As I was choosing my favorites, there it appeared, a picture of Mark in living color. I gasped. Wow! He is so handsome. "Wait, Agnes, stop right there, dismiss any notions of romance," I told myself. If there was a brief something or could be a something, it was over before it began. The story of my love life.

chapter six

All set for my morning hike. The tour guide had my hiking boots waiting for me. I was not sure if there would be thick forest to trudge through so I wore long sleeves and long pants in hopes to escape scratches and possible wounds. I knew I was over dramatizing the outing but I was nervous. I kept telling myself, "Agnes, this is supposed to be fun." But I was not listening to my own cheer section. Visions of thorny bushes and snakes hiding in the leaves fogged my mind. The rest of the group seemed energized ready to hit the trail. There were three trail choices; easy, intermediate and skilled. As you might guess, I chose easy trail.

After about an hour of hiking stopping for a break, I see the hikers from the intermediate and skilled trails emerge. Everyone greeted one another again sharing some quick hiking highlights. Then, the tour guides lead everyone to an equipment tent announcing, "It is time to gear up for the zip line." I surely thought I misheard the announcement. I don't zip line. There was no mention of a zip line in the brochure that I recall. Now I am frantic. I stutter, "Surely, there is another way down."

The guide shares as he points, "You can take that path on the right. It will lead you back to our starting location."

"Ok, great, I will see you there," and I started walking, almost running.

Then the guide shares the rest of the story. "That route takes over 6 hours, across dangerous terrain."

I stopped in my tracks. What! You mean it is zip line or no life. These are my choices. Fine. I geared up taking my place at the end of the line. Tourist after tourist went whistling down the line at warp speed. Waiting and watching, I died a thousand deaths. Now I regret not being first in line then I would be finished by now. I think I am finished anyway. Oh help! Anyone, help!

"Hi, Grace. Would you like a zip line partner?"

Now I am hearing the zip line angels and saints coming to whisk me up to heaven. I have heard it preached many times, "Be vigilante. You never know the hour nor the day." Preparing for death, I turn around and in astonishment I realize it is Mark offering to help me down the mountain. Now I am really in shock! Barely able to speak, I stammer a feeble, "Please."

I was gasping for air once we landed at the bottom. Eyes closed, I kicked and screamed all the way down. I am sure Mark will be hard of hearing the rest of his life on his left side. I regret being such a baby. The tour guides gave me disgruntled looks. I doubt if I will be invited back for more hiking ventures. They don't seem to even want me to return their boots. I think my screaming behavior sent away potential customers.

"Now that we lived through that expedition, would you like to relax and get something to drink?"

Mark always seems to know exactly what to say and when to say it. On the other hand, I can only manage a weak, "Sure."

Nervous from the "near death" zip line experience combined with elation from my knight in shining zip-line armor rescuing me, I drank my drinks too fast. I had convinced myself I would never see Mark again since my money pocket slip of the tongue comment. Yet, here he was back in my life again. My head was spinning even faster than before when I was flying through the mountain jungle. Out I go. I am telling myself, "Agnes, Agnes, wake up!" But my eyes would not open. My body would not move. This is really the end.

chapter seven

I feel the warmth of the sun on my face. I smell the delicious aroma of coffee in the air. I open one eye and quickly close it again from the glare of the sun. Oh, I hurt all over, my head, my arms, my legs, even my face.

I am supposed to be on a vacation getting rejuvenated, not feel like I have been run over by a Mack truck.

"Good morning, sleepy-head."

Did I just hear Mark's voice? Oh my, where am I? What has happened?

"Let me help you sit-up."

I am afraid to speak.

Just wait and maybe he will explain.

"You had a big day, yesterday."

Yesterday? I hope this story unfolds in my favor.

"Drinks after the hiking and zip line adventure got the best of you."

It did?

I am still afraid to speak so I just listen.

"Some friends helped me get you safely to my rental so you could rest."

They did? And…

"That's it. You slept, now you are awake."

That's it. I slept, now I am awake. Thank goodness.

"I owe you a huge thank you. Thank you!"

"I am always happy to help a damsel in distress!"

He thinks of me as a damsel, but in distress. This may be good and bad.

Mark hands me a cup of coffee. "Thank you. I will have a few sips then I best be going. I know you must have important things to do today other than watch over me."

"My calendar happens to be completely clear."

"Ok, well I best be on my way just because…"

Just because…

"If you are game, I would love to drive you around the area and show you some fantastic photography sights."

I really wanted to accept Mark's offer. However, I did not really know what day it was. My head was very cloudy. My thoughts very jumbled. Trying to think of a clever comeback I chuckle saying, "As far as I can remember, I believe my calendar is clear today, too." We both laugh and smile at each other.

"I will take you to your cottage then come back for you around 10:00. Sound good?"

"Perfect, thank you."

I guess? I think? I hope?

chapter eight

Spending the day with Mark was out of this world spectacular. He showed me the most picturesque views. I took twice as many pictures in the same amount of time as Mark. With my camera set on "A" I was click, click, click while he was focus this, aperture that. I can't wait to compare pictures. I bet my automatic photos are just as good or better.

Agnes, this is not the time to show your competitive nature.

Mark was so thoughtful. He brought a picnic lunch we shared beside a beautiful waterfall. He poured us glasses of wine. I enjoyed every sip but paced myself. I didn't want any more embarrassing events. To watch the sunset, we parked on top of the hillside looking over the water. I was so relaxed enjoying the company I was with and the beautiful surroundings.

As we drove back to my cottage, we were both quiet just taking in the delights of the day. I was also thankful during the day there had been no mention of my zip-line hazard night, my money pocket comment or any of my previous mishaps.

Mark was quite the gentleman. He walked me to my door. We thanked each other for a terrific day. Mark offered to take our film to get it developed at the photo shop. Mark kissed me gently on the cheek, walked back to his car and drove away. I think I was in shell shock. I stood at my front door for 15 minutes or more trying to decipher what just happened. Mark kissed me, on the cheek but he kissed me. It counts in my book.

chapter nine

Walking around on Cloud 9 without a care in the world I thought this vacation is turning out all right. I am relaxed, seeing some breathtaking sights, taking awesome "automatic" photos and may have found the love of my life. I have spent day after day exploring special retreat sights with Mark. We start with breakfast on the beach. The bakery in town has delicious fresh pastries daily and the fruit stand next door to the bakery has mouth-watering melons and berries. We take turns packing a picnic lunch. I usually pack salads and a surprise dessert for us. Mark brings cheese and crackers with paired bottles of wine. He says the wine is our dessert. I don't argue but I wonder.

How does he know so much about wines?

I admire that knowledge. I am not a wine connoisseur but I do have some favorites. Back home after work on Fridays, I meet some co-workers at a bar near the office. I usually order a glass of Pinot Grigio. I sip away the week enjoying the cool, crisp wine. At home on Saturday nights, I treat myself to a glass of Chianti as I splurge calories on a deli pizza. Honestly, any wine label of any year taste good to me.

There are countless evening dining places to choose with a variety of menus at paradise retreat. We have tried a different restaurant every evening. "Grace" has tried shrimp, lobster, salmon, even an oyster or two. Oysters, were not my favorite. I was afraid to chew, so I just swallowed and smiled.

At the end of each day, Mark always drives us back to my cottage, walks me to the door, slowly takes me in his arms and kisses me with passion, desire, emotion, bringing forth the woman in me. My body tingles to my toes. I melt away into an everlasting love. I watch Mark saunter back to his car and drive away yet I am not able to move. I stand in the doorway, my head spinning with glee thinking of a wonderful life ahead.

chapter ten

Mark announced, "This is my last day at paradise retreat. I will be returning home in the morning. Let's make this a day we will always remember." Hearing his words, I was mixed with emotions. Happy we are spending this precious time together yet saddened that the end is near.

Or is it the end? Is there a future for Mark and "Grace", I mean Agnes? Oh, what a mess I have created.

True to Mark's words, we made it a day we would never forget. We filled every minute of the day creating moments of laughter and pure joy as we splashed each other with the incoming waves. We took a private horseback ride on the beach. I teamed up with Wildfire again. Mark rode Zorro. Zorro like Wildfire was a beautiful animal. Zorro true to his name had a brilliant black coat, black mane and tail. Zorro's eyes were so dark, they appeared black. As magnificent as Zorro was, I figured Wildfire was faster since she was a mustang. So, guess which horse and rider got drenched racing back to the barn. Not Wildfire and me.

Sometimes my competitive nature comes in handy.

We made a campfire on the beach cooking fish and shrimp for lunch. Mark brought a special wine he insisted was the perfect wine to boost the flavor of the seafood. I can say it was all delicious. Exhausted from the ride and relaxed from the wine, now stuffed from eating too much, we snuggled under the palm trees listening to a gentle breeze blowing by. Before falling asleep, Mark gave me a sweet kiss on my forehead and said, "Grace, I love you!"

Was that the wine talking or Mark talking?

Oh my! Did I hear what I think I heard? I am laying in his arms, knowing there is nowhere on the earth I would rather be. I need to tell him that I love him, too. But I didn't say anything.

Why didn't I say anything?

Back at the cottage, Mark says, "I have special dinner plans for us. I will pick you up in an hour."

"Should I wear an evening gown?" I was joking.

"Sundress and a wrap should be perfect."

I had the perfect sundress I had been saving for a special paradise occasion. It was red and white polka dot with a tie waist and spaghetti straps. I decided to pull my hair up which helped frame my face. I placed a gold barrette on the side that matched my gold necklace. As I clasped my necklace around my neck, it reminded me of the gold chain Mark was always wearing. Mark's chain had a gold circular pendant with the letter "L" engraved on it.

I wonder what the "L" stands for, probably his middle name?"

The surprise dinner was a sunset sailing cruise. Oh, what a night, a perfect night. The water was calm but there was a nice breeze filling the sails as we floated along the shoreline watching the sun set on the horizon. Our dinner, Mark ordered in advance. We had crab cake appetizers, fresh fruit salads, surf and turf entrees. For dessert, Mark knew I love chocolate anything so I had molten lave cake and he had lemon cheesecake. And a habit of Mark's I was quickly growing accustomed to, a wine paired with each dinner course. I should have been counting, there were four pairings plus an after-dinner sherry Mark called a "digestif."

After my "digestif," I was very relaxed and rather sleepy. So was Mark. Once the boat was docked, we decided to stay the night on the boat. We laid in each other's arms, looking at the stars as we dozed off into a deep slumber.

chapter eleven

On his way to the airport, Mark came by the cottage. We didn't want to say good-bye but we knew we had life's obligations to separately attend to. Standing by the water's edge, Mark held me close. Mark looked at me for a moment as if he wanted to tell me something but didn't. He kissed me once, he kissed me twice, he kissed me once again. We both didn't want our memorable time together to end. With one last hug good-bye, Mark got in his car and began to drive away. Almost out of sight, looking back Mark yells to me, "Grace, I love you."

Mark, I love you, too. I need to tell him how I feel? Oh no! He called me Grace. Oh no! He doesn't even know my name. Oh no! I will never see him again?

I yelled, "Mark, I love you. My name is really Agnes, Agnes Brown." He was too far away to hear me. It was too late. Mark was gone, gone forever.

The tears began to stream down my face.

✱✱✱

My last few days of vacation, I tried to relive my days with Mark. I revisited the beautiful tropical sights I shared with Mark. In my mind, I would have conversations with Mark as if he were there. I had so many questions to ask him: Where do you live? What family business do you manage? Do you have siblings? When is your birthday? I was not sure if this behavior was mentally healthy. But, pretending to talk to Mark gave me moments of comfort then the tears would begin to flow again. I did not want to accept the fact but, in my heart, I knew my love, my life with Mark, would never come to be. The tears began to flow, and flow, and flow.

chapter twelve

So here I am again, forty years later needing a life restoration. I tried to remember years ago if there was something I did that helped me go forward from my loss. Years ago, I was trying to mend my broken heart. I admit my heart has always remained broken. With a simple thought of Mark, I feel weak inside. Falling in love with Mark then never seeing him again truly devastated me. I wondered if he tried to find me. Then I reminded myself: How could he? He didn't know my real name. The one-time Agnes let her hair down, becoming Grace Brownley has haunted me 'til this day.

My paradise retreat meeting Mark, falling in love, dreaming of my love, my life with Mark changed my life in a beautiful way. But, returning home and not being able to find him or he find me left my life an empty stage, a life forgone.

I cried for days, leading into months, then years. But my heart ache remained. My logical mind told me I was holding onto memories that would never set me free. I knew I needed to stop looking at my paradise retreat photo album twenty times a day, especially since I put Mark's photograph on the cover. I knew the best action for me to take was to pack all of those memories away in the suitcase where they came from, never to be opened again. So, I did.

To fill the continued emptiness I felt inside, I ramped up my work load and forced myself to attend social events with friends. In fact, trying to busy my day keeping my mind from dwelling on lost love, I agreed to go to the BBQ cook-off with my neighbors. That was the day I met Hank.

chapter thirteen

Now facing the loss of Hank, the man I shared more than half of my life with, I am still searching for my path leading to joy and happiness. Living in the mountains is definitely helping. Having Rusty at my side is very comforting. But I am still so sad inside. My heart still aches.

I have tried changing my appearance. I have smelled like a smokehouse for too long. In fact, I never wanted to hurt Hank's feelings so I never told him, I really don't like BBQ, eating it or cooking it. Trying to rid myself of smokehouse smells, I cut my hair very short and I have scrubbed my skin with every perfume soap I can find. I filled my mountain home with potpourri. Rusty seems to enjoy the fresh smells. I know I do.

It took a while for me to unpack and settle into my mountain home. Looking around the house one day I saw only one box left to unpack. Hallelujah! Sipping my hot cocoa, I sat down to open the box. Toward the bottom of the box, I found the paradise retreat suitcase I tucked away so many years ago.

Do I dare open it? Will the memories come flowing back of joy or tragedy?

I closed the box quickly, pushed it to the side and went outside to play with Rusty. After all of these years, I cannot face such hurt again. As ridiculous as it may seem, it has taken me decades to forgive myself for not telling Mark that I loved him, that I wanted to share my life with him, that I never wanted to be a day without him and that my name was Agnes Brown, not Grace Brownley.

Oh Agnes, you were such a fool!

No, I will not open that suitcase and look at the photo album. I am not ready.

Agnes, really? It has been over forty years.

No, I can't return to that darkness. Forty years or not, unfortunately I am not strong enough, not yet.

chapter fourteen

My first winter in the mountains went by swiftly. Rusty was great company through the snowy days. I am thankful for me and for Rusty, the Morrisons let Rusty stay in the mountains. Rusty loves the snow. I enjoyed watching him run and play in the snow piles, as I stayed bundled from head to foot. The strong cold air seemed refreshing to him. It was rather startling to me. Watching him enjoy his surroundings helped me see and feel the beauty. I hope Rusty is not too disappointed now that the snow is melting. I can see some sprigs of green grass sprouting around the sides of the house.

I received a flyer in the mail advertising a spring festival in town. I thought it was time Rusty and I met "the neighbors." Springtime in the mountains is still rather cool. I bundled up, hooked Rusty to his leash and off we went.

I really love the town. It is small and quaint, no hustle and bustle. Although, this day there was an upbeat vibe with the festival activities taking place. The locals were selling their wares and trinkets they created during the winter months. I had thought about doing some writing. I used to write articles advertising HG's BBQ for the newspaper and a few magazines back in Kansas. At the time, it was fun. Now, thinking of writing, reminded me of what I had traveled far to forget. So, I dismissed the idea for the time being. When I write, I want to be inspired writing about exciting and interesting topics.

Rusty and I walked up and down the rows. I thought I might purchase some fresh potpourri for the house and get Rusty some new toys. It still may be a while before we find his old toys. He hid most in the snow about two feet deep. It is going to take a few more months before all the snow melts.

Rusty and I made our purchases then, went to the burger café for a bite to eat. My burger was delicious. Rusty enjoyed his burger treat as well. I must say, I don't think it is my imagination. I believe food taste better in the mountains or I am finally getting my taste buds restored from years of eating BBQ. Totally satisfied with our eating and shopping, Rusty and I headed for home.

With spring approaching it was time for some spring cleaning. The house could use some fresh air before I set out the fresh potpourri. I opened the windows and began dusting the furniture. I spied the one box left unpacked. As Rusty ran around the yard, I sat on the porch wrapped in a blanket and slowly opened the box removing the suitcase holding the treasured photo album.

Immediately, I see the photo of Mark on the cover.

Looking at the photo took me back to that moment. I remember he walked up to me while I was sitting on the beach taking photos of the sunset (on automatic) and sipping my Shirley Temple. He asked if he could sit with me. He introduced himself saying, "Mark, Mark Stoneleigh." I could not stop staring at the photo. He was so good looking. I wonder if age has treated him well. I guess I will never know.

Looking through the rest of the album, I remember how much I enjoyed taking the photos, especially the photos of the engaging scenery. I began rapidly digging through the remaining items in the box. There it was, my old Minolta camera. These days, I know everyone uses their mobile phone cameras to take their pictures. I know whether on automatic or not, these cameras of yesteryear deliver precise, crisp images. I announced to myself, "Agnes, it is time for you to graduate from automatic to reality."

The next day, Rusty and I venture to town. Our first stop, the Turning Pages Bookshop. Pets are welcome in all of the town stores, so Rusty and I went in looking for the "How to …" section. Gladys, the shop owner was a retired teacher. She gladly directed us to the back of the store offering help if needed. Studying the selections, I made my choice, "How to Focus."

Our second stop, Mac's Photo Shop. The youngster behind the counter politely kept from laughing as he viewed my camera. He called his grandfather I assumed was Mac, from the back room to come assist. Their store did not stock the particular film I needed but we placed an order for a box of 12 rolls of film, 24 exposures per roll. I figured almost 300 shots would give me a good start. We were able to schedule the film to be delivered to my home. Perfect! I was excited to get home and begin learning "How to Focus."

Within a few weeks, I knew how to set the aperture, shutter speed and "ISO" settings allowing the perfect amount of light to enter the camera. Then you focus, and click. I was thinking as I improve, to add some variation, I would buy a zoom lens and possibly a wide-angle lens.

Now mid-summer, the foothills were intermixed with long blades of green grass and multi-colored wild flowers. Rusty and I strolled along the mountain's edge capturing shots of bumble bees nourishing on sweet nectar. Rusty would rustle through the grass stirring a nest of doves. At first, I was not quit fast enough setting the this and that needed and then focus to get the shot. I admit I was tempted to switch to automatic. But fighting the urge, I trudged on. There were a few wasted shots. I chalked those up to my learning curve.

Fall arrived with my photography improving daily. I challenged myself to catch the perfect lighting showing the color changes surrounding me. Rusty enjoyed our photo sessions then taking the film into town to the photo shop. Mac would send the film to a shop set-up with the special processing equipment required to develop the photographs. Rusty and I picked up the developed photos every Tuesday, had our favorite burger at the Burger Café, then hurried home for more photography sessions. I guess you could say I had no off switch when it came to photography. I called myself "The Accidental Photographer."

During the winter months, for me, it took a lot of bundling and fortitude venturing into the cold to photograph. However, Rusty, being a Bernese Mountain dog, delighted in every snow bank he could pounce. Rusty was my main subject, truthfully, my only subject to photograph. He had so many different facial (muzzle) expressions. I captured a few shots as he shook sending snow flying in every direction, usually leaving me covered in wet. I needed to figure out how to take that wet selfie or maybe not.

By the end of spring, I had accumulated photographs of a year in the mountains. As I displayed the photos around the house; on the kitchen counters, dining room table, coffee and end tables, my desk, I decided to create a photography book. Rusty would be the star feature of course. Depending, I might venture into self-publishing.

chapter fifteen

Within a few months, I finished the layout of the photography book. I didn't realize how many photos I had taken. I do know I enjoyed the time I spent learning and trying to master the art. Now was the moment of truth. I decided to show the book to Gladys at Turning Pages Bookshop. I knew Gladys would give my book an honest review. I titled the book, *Clarity – from Automatic to Aperture and Focus*. To be true to the title, I showed photos from my paradise retreat from years ago taken on "automatic" beside photos I took using manual settings. I used my favorite photographs of Rusty on the covers. On the front cover, I placed a photograph of Rusty bouncing through the snow. On the back cover, I used a photograph of Rusty running for his life after disturbing a bumble bee's lunch.

I dedicated *Clarity* in memory of Hank, my beloved husband and to my beautiful daughters and families. I gave acknowledgments to my super friends at Turning Pages Bookshop and Mac's Photo Shop. Their expertise made *Clarity* a reality. I recognized the paradise retreat;

where beautiful scenery awaits a camera lens. Going out on a limb yet coming straight from my heart I noted in my acknowledgments, Mark Stoneleigh; a Love, a Life, Forgone with only these few photographs of remembrance.

In addition, on the back cover, along with a short bio, to give proper credits, I placed a picture of myself from the paradise retreat with my alias name, Grace Brownley underneath and a picture of myself, present day with the name Agnes Brown Gray underneath.

Gladys loved the photography book. She said she wanted to show it to some of her retired teacher friends. I agreed. You never know.

Rusty and I came to town a few weeks later to replenish photography supplies and to dine on our favorite burgers. As we were leaving town, I decided to check in with Gladys.

Gladys was behind the counter when we walked into the bookstore. Gladys jumped up, face beaming, "It is great to see you. I am so happy you stopped by."

"Thank you. It is nice seeing you, too."

"I have exciting news. I didn't bother to contact you with details earlier. My friends and I decided *Clarity* had to be published so I shared your wonderful photography book with a longtime teacher friend of mine, Ross Mason. Ross' family has a well-known publishing company that has been in business for years. Ross reviewed *Clarity* and said their company would be delighted to publish if you were in agreement."

My heart is pounding out of my chest hearing Gladys' news. Rusty innately recognizes my excitement and starts barking and jumping up and down. "Yes, yes!" Hearing this news makes the best day of my life next to my wedding day and the birthing days of my three daughters. Gladys told me to get started, Ross needed particular files in certain formats. Luckily, I understood what she meant and I actually had the files on my computer. Gladys gave me Ross' email and I told her I would send the files as soon as Rusty and I got home.

Publishing my book, now I am an "Accidental Author!"

chapter sixteen

While waiting for *Clarity* to be published, Rusty and I returned to our daily walk abouts and I continued taking photographs. Every day I found many beautiful engaging scenes I enjoyed capturing on film to later revisit. If I ever stopped to count, I am sure I took at least 20 shots of Rusty enthralled in his antics each day.

It was a cold morning so I had bundled heavily before Rusty and I went out to photograph. When we got home, as I was removing many layers of clothing, I noticed my answering machine light was blinking. I thought this was strange. Since the few years I had been living in the mountains, I never remember having a message. Before listening, I made some hot cocoa then noticed my computer light flashing showing emails awaited. I had turned off the ringer to my mobile phone while Rusty and I were out exploring. I checked my mobile phone to see a list of missed calls.

What is going on?

Since the light blinking on the answering machine was the most mysterious, I decided to check the machine first.

"You have three messages," the machine recited. First message: "Mom, this is Lucy, your first born. Why didn't you tell us you were into photography? You published a book! Who is Mark Stoneleigh?"

Second message: "Mom, this is Lacey. You are a photographer and a published author. Awesome. Who is Mark Stoneleigh?"

Third message: "Mom, this is Lexie. I am so proud of you. What an amazing book. The photographs seem so real. Who is Mark Stoneleigh?"

Oh my, what is going on?

Checking my mobile phone next, it appeared Lucy, Lacey and Lexie had also called my mobile phone. I opened my computer and began reading numerous emails. The first three emails were from the girls. The next email was from Gladys asking me to come to the bookshop as soon as possible. The next email was from Ross saying he believed *Clarity* will be the next best seller.

I snuggled with Rusty on the sofa finishing my hot cocoa trying to gather my thoughts. I was excited to hear Ross predicted *Clarity* to be the next best seller but my mind was wrapped around the girls asking, "Who is Mark Stoneleigh?"

Who is Mark Stoneleigh?

Before returning the girls' phone calls, I needed to answer the question myself, "Who is Mark Stoneleigh?" Do I admit Mark was the love of my life I lost (because of my stupidity)? Do I go on to admit … stop? Lucy, Lacey, and Lexie have only known of my love for their father. My life before Hank is for my heart only.

Now, I wish I would have kept this unknown love, unknown life my secret hidden from the world forever.

I thought I best get to town to see Gladys as soon as possible. Thinking to arrive incognito, I bundled adding extra scarves, hats and glasses and left Rusty taking his morning nap on his comfy pillow.

I suppose I fooled no one. Gladys immediately recognized me. "Agnes, quick come see!"

I couldn't believe it. Gladys held up a copy of *Clarity*.

"Agnes, your book is here. It is absolutely stunning."

Gladys hands me my book. I did it. I published a book. Wow! So many emotions were running through my head, my body. I felt a little faint. Gladys saw me turning white. She offered me a chair and some water. I sat down catching my breath and began looking at my *Clarity*. The photographs of Rusty on the covers were fantastic. My hands were shaking with joy and excitement looking at each page, the colors of the photographs were so vivid. Ross' family publishing company had wonderful printing capabilities that brought each photograph to life. Oh, I love my book. It is more than I could even imagine. I gave *Clarity* a huge hug.

Coming back to reality for a moment, I looked at Gladys and asked, "Have you shown *Clarity* to anyone else?"

"No, I wanted you to see it first!"

"Well somehow my daughters and many others seem to have seen *Clarity*."

"Well, I happened to post the covers and a few pages of *Clarity* on Turning Pages Bookshop's social media."

"What? Social media! Oh my! Did you happen to post the acknowledgment page?"

"Of course."

Now I understand why the girls asked, "Who is Mark Stoneleigh?" A question I don't have an answer for.

chapter seventeen

Leighton Winery – Southern California

Marc Leighton was making his morning rounds of the vast vineyards of the Leighton Winery. The Leighton family was hoping their Cabernet Sauvignon would receive a gold medal from the Global Cabernet Sauvignon Masters this year. For the first time in a long time, the weather cooperated producing delicious Cabernet Franc and Cabernet Blanc grapes yielding a fruity, full-bodied Cab. Everyone was excited, yet anxious.

This morning, taking a few minutes, resting in the shade of the vines, Marc's mind traveled back to his favorite paradise retreat, to the year he met a precious girl named Grace, Grace Brownley. He and Grace shared the beauty of the paradise retreat, taking photographs of the tropical flowers and trees with the backdrop of the waterfalls and the sea. Marc chuckled remembering Grace always took her pictures on the automatic setting of her camera. She was special. Marc remembered their afternoon picnics, and especially their last night together. A beautiful dinner sailing along the shoreline. He remembered the sparkle in her eyes, such innocence and purity. Marc had fallen in love.

To Marc, Grace was the breath of fresh air of the paradise retreat. He remembered rescuing Grace from the zip line. Matter of fact, after all of these years he still finds it difficult to hear out of his left ear. Grace was a joy!

Marc was heart-broken when their romance ended so abruptly. He tried to find her after he returned home but he knew very little about her, only her name and that she worked in mergers. He wanted to tell her that his name was really Marc Leighton. He made it a habit to travel with an alias. It saved from people recognizing him and asking him to taste and rate their wines. That year, that trip, he wished he had used his real name. He didn't know he was to meet the love of his life. A Love, A Life, Forgone.

As silly as it may seem, for years Marc returned to the paradise retreat passing the cottage Grace had rented. He even made sure he went the same month of the year hoping she would return. Unfortunately, Mark never saw Grace again which saddens him to this very day.

When Marc returned to the winery showroom he glanced at a book of photography on the tasting bar. He thought, what a unique title, *Clarity – From Automatic to Aperture and Focus*. As he thumbed through a few pages, he recognized scenes in the photographs, scenes of paradise retreat. Marc quickly turned to the back cover.

Grace, my Grace Brownley. No, it is Agnes, Agnes Brown Gray. What?

chapter eighteen

Returning home from the bookshop, I rousted Rusty from his nap to show him *Clarity*. Rusty responded with several barks of approval. I knew I could not procrastinate any longer. I needed to call the girls. Before I left the bookshop, Gladys scheduled book signings in the upcoming months. Gladys explained book signings were a terrific way to showcase *Clarity* so I agreed. I thought it would be fun to invite the girls and their families to a book signing. Maybe that will take their mind off of the "Who is Mark Stoneleigh?" question and I can defer an answer.

It worked. The girls are excited to come to my book signing. Wow! All are coming; Lucy, Clark, and Carter; Lacey, Wayne, and Henry; Lexie, Niccolò with Ricardo, Lorenzo and Antonio. Oh my, Rusty. We have to get ready. We are not used to having guests. I am totally not ready; book signings, guests.

Maybe I should have stayed on automatic. Clarity is proving to be very transparent.

Gladys scheduled the book signing for a Saturday morning. Lucy, Lacey, Lexie and families had arrived for the big event. Rusty was in overdrive romping with all of the kids. They were all playing hard and sleeping well. I, on the other hand, was finding it difficult to sleep. I was really excited. Me, a photographer and an author. Yea! In the past, I attended a few book signings so I knew the sequence of events. But it was hard for me to imagine people were actually coming to see me and thank me for the photographs and the book. Wow!

Oh, a moment of panic, I hope someone shows up. What if I don't sign any books? I will embarrass my family and friends.

It was book signing day. I left for the bookshop early. I wanted to help Gladys prepare the tables and books. I thought it best to enter from the back door. As I circled the block to park in the back, I was somewhat relieved. There were people already in line out front.

As I suspected, Gladys was miles ahead of me in preparations. Clarity was displayed in the bookshop windows, on tables and shelves. Gladys had pastries, coffee and refreshments available for all to enjoy.

At 10:00 am, Gladys looked at me and asked, "Agnes, are you ready?"

"I suppose as ready as I ever will be."

Gladys opened the doors and the bookshop instantly was filled with people, young and old. Gladys told me after someone purchased Clarity then they would come to my table for my autograph. Sounded easy enough. Oh my! For hours I don't believe I lifted my head. I was signing one book after another. I never knew there were so many people all with different names. I never wrote: To Mary, To John, … twice. I am not sure why I found that so intriguing but it was.

Gladys had advertised the book signing to be a two-hour event. Two hours had passed and there were still people in line. Gladys looked over at me with questioning eyes. I looked back giving her the thumbs up sign. Let's keep going. Well into the afternoon, I looked at Gladys this time hand signaling the question, "Do we have enough books?" Gladys gave me the thumbs up sign, so she kept selling and I kept signing.

With my head down ready to sign, I hear a gentleman say, "Would you please autograph the book to Marc? That is Marc with a "c" not a "k.""

Oh, my goodness. I recognize that voice. Do I dare look up?

I slowly raise my head. First, I see a memorable gold chain and pendant.

Could it really be Mark, after all of these years? Do I dare raise my eyes higher?

Then raising my eyes higher, I see Mark Stoneleigh. My head is spinning. I drop my pen. We both reach down at the same time to pick it up. Looking into those same beautiful blue eyes of yesteryears I stutter asking, "Did you say with a "c", not a "k?""

"Will you be signing as Grace Brownley or Agnes Brown Gray?"

I never answer, I never sign, I just collapse into his arms.

chapter nineteen

When I come to, I search the room for Mark or Marc. It doesn't matter how he spells his name. I actually was with him again after all of these years. Or was I? Was this all a dream? I pinch myself making sure I was alive. "Ouch!"

I am surrounded by Gladys, Lucy, Lacey and Lexie, all four, in unison, blasting me with questions. "Are you alright?" "Who was that man? Was that Mark? Why did you faint?" Not seeing Marc anywhere, my heart is sinking not knowing if Marc was gone forever, again? Still feeling dizzy, I ask to be driven home as I hold back my tears.

The next morning, assured I was feeling better, everyone gathered their belongings and departed in different directions. The grand-boys tried to pack Rusty, but I rescued him in the nick of time. I am waving goodbye as Rusty barks goodbye. As Rusty and I wave seeing the last car going down the drive, another car is coming up. At first, I figured one of the grand-kids left a toy, or night-night or something. But, as the car nears, I don't recognize it. The car parks at the top of the drive. I steady myself grabbing the stair handrail as I see it is Marc.

As Marc gets out of the car, I wanted to run to him smothering him with hugs and kisses, never stopping.

Agnes, wait. Do you want to scare him away? Agnes, think slow and easy, slow and easy. It has been over forty years. Remember, the last, last time you saw him a few days ago, you collapsed.

Holding onto Rusty for moral support, I invite Marc in. I can't stop looking at him. I know it has been many years, but it feels like the first moment I met him when I tapped him on the shoulder and asked him the name of his drink. Marc sees the paradise retreat photograph album (with his picture on the cover) on the coffee table next to *Clarity*. He looks at a few pages and asks, "You don't take automatic photos anymore?"

"No, I graduated to manual settings."

We look at each other and laugh, forty years of laughs that soon turn to tears.

"Why, Grace, I mean Agnes, why did you use a different name on your vacation when we met?"

"The only answer I have is that I was being silly. I have never liked my name Agnes. So, I thought for once in my life I would go by a name I love which is Grace. I didn't know that my silliness would cause me to lose the love of my life."

"I only knew your name, Mark Stoneleigh. I didn't know where you lived or even your birthday."

"I have to confess to being silly as well. On that vacation and all of my previous travels, I used a different name so no one would know me. You see my family is well-known for its winery. My name is really Marc Leighton of Leighton Wineries in California."

"No wonder I never could find you. I am sorry for both of us that we are now just learning each other's real names. Please, if you have time, I would love to visit and learn of the forty years we missed sharing together."

I noticed Rusty was very much at ease sitting beside Marc. I offered to share my story first, of meeting Hank and the years running HG's BBQ smokehouse. I started to tell him about girls and their families. He said they did not know who he was but he visited with them at the book signing.

"Grace, no I mean, Agnes, what name would you like for me to call you?"

"Grace!"

"Then, Grace it is. Grace, I thought your family was beautiful and I could tell they love and admire you immensely!"

"Thank you, Marc with a "c.""

Marc told me he never married. He said his sister is married and has two sons. Marc said he is very close to his nephews. His nephews call him Uncle Daddy. Marc said his family business keeps him busy. He explained every year it is very competitive amongst the wineries. It is important to have an award-winning wine, year to year in order to keep a steady customer base.

From the BBQ business, I understood the importance of serving award-winning BBQ and BBQ sauce enticing customers to return.

Marc and I started looking at *Clarity* and the past photograph album. Marc says, "I went back year after year to the paradise retreat at the same time of year hoping I would see you as I drove by the cottage." I felt my heart break all over again. I began to cry. If I only would have known.

Sobbing I ask, "After all of this time, how did you find me?"

"Here." Marc pointed to my pictures and names on the back cover of *Clarity*.

Tears streaming down my face, I hold him tightly, "I was hoping by some miracle you would see me and you did. Thank goodness for *Clarity*."

Marc returns the hug. "Grace, I would love to share the rest of my life with you. I have always loved you." He kisses me. His warm, gentle lips feel the same as the first time we kissed. Long, lost beautiful memories stream through my mind. I feel my life begin again as Mark takes my hand.

"My Love, My Life, Forever is Yours!"

acknowledgments

My family and friends for their everlasting love, support, and encouragement.

My newest friend and awesome graphic designer. Thank you, Gaby.

about the author

Renee Goodwin is an award-winning author of GG Life Lesson Storybook Series ® books. Renee has an undying passion for education which began at an early age. Through the years Renee has become an accomplished teacher, engineer, businesswoman, author and artist.

Renee is the recipient of the 2021 Texas A&M University Aggie Women Legacy award. She continues her legacy with her GG Life Lesson Storybook Series ® books on exhibit at the Cushing Library at Texas A&M University.

Renee created her own publishing company, Goodwin Global Publishing, LLC offering authors professional contract publishing services producing quality products while establishing loyal and long-term relationships.

Renee offers GG Life Lesson Storybook Series ® books for purchase on her website, personally autographed and mailed to you.

Renee is happy to announce *A Love, A Life, Forgone* is one of two novels she is publishing in 2022 with *Living Past Shadows* her other novel. Renee looks forward to publishing more novels in the future for reader enjoyment.